MW00995430

MY LIFE IS WEIRD!

MY DAD IS A UNICORN!

WRITTEN BY **BILL CANTERBURY**   ILLUSTRATED BY **JEFF HARTER**

Doubleday Books for Young Readers

Most dads are weird.

They tell bad jokes.

What's a squirrel's favorite number? Tree!

Text copyright © 2025 by Bill Canterbury • Cover art and interior illustrations copyright © 2025 by Jeff Harter • All rights reserved. Published in the United States by Doubleday, an imprint of Random House Children's Books, a division of Penguin Random House LLC, 1745 Broadway, New York, NY 10019. • DOUBLEDAY YR with colophon is a registered trademark of Penguin Random House LLC. • Visit us on the Web! rhcbooks.com • Educators and librarians, for a variety of teaching tools, visit us at RHTeachersLibrarians.com • Library of Congress Cataloging-in-Publication Data is available upon request. • ISBN 978-0-593-80787-3 (trade) — ISBN 978-0-593-80788-0 (lib. bdg.) — ISBN 978-0-593-80789-7 (ebook) • MANUFACTURED IN CHINA • 10 9 8 7 6 5 4 3 2 1 • First Edition
Random House Children's Books supports the First Amendment and celebrates the right to read.

Or they cheer for teams you've never heard of.

Let's go, DENVER DOORBELLS! Ding-dong, bing-bong!

Or they read tool catalogs for fun.

These hammers are from heaven!

Well, *my dad is REALLY weird,* because my dad is a . . .

UNICORN!

Having a unicorn for a dad sounds super fun, right?
All cookies and cakes and magical muffins?

Well, it's not!
My unicorn dad . . .

Gets his necktie stuck
around his horn . . .

Little help,
please?

Practices his prancing at midnight . . .

And is obsessed with
his new mane shampoo.

Even worse, he leaves glitter EVERYWHERE!

Like when the pipe broke . . .

And when the car wouldn't start . . .

And when I needed help with my homework.

Sometimes my dad has to go solve unicorn problems in magical lands.

It was my first mission ever with my dad!

Some mean goblins had come to Candy Cane Canyon!

They were ruining the unicorns' favorite game!

The week after, my dad brought me on an even scarier mission to Merrymuffin Meadows! Trolls were stealing the unicorns' giant lollipop!

And one day, Dad and I went together to Starrycake Sugarfalls
to solve the SCARIEST PROBLEM EVER!

A fire-breathing dragon was eating all the unicorns' marshmallows!

We got away just in time and headed home for our usual celebration . . .

LASAGNA!

Okay, sometimes it *is* fun that my dad is a unicorn.

We play Hula Hoop together.

He lets me use his fancy mane shampoo.

He always gets me to school on time.

EVERY DAY IS UNICORN DAY!

CLUB UNICORN

UNICORN!

BORN A UNICORN

I'M A UNICORN DAD

GLITTERIFIC!

TEAM UNICORN

KER-SPARKLE!

GLITTER

I Make RAINBOWS!

KA-POW!

Rainbows Forever!

TEAM GLITTER

BEST DAD!

GLITTER SQUAD

BEST DAD!

WELCOME TO GLITTER TOWN!

GLITTER KA—BANG